PRIMROSE DAY

By Carolyn Haywood

"B" IS FOR BETSY
BETSY AND BILLY
BACK TO SCHOOL WITH BETSY
BETSY AND THE BOYS
HERE'S A PENNY
PENNY AND PETER
PRIMROSE DAY
TWO AND TWO ARE FOUR

Primrose Day

Written and Illustrated
by
Carolyn Haywood

A Voyager/HBJ Book
HARCOURT BRACE JOVANOVICH, PUBLISHERS
San Diego New York London

Library of Congress Cataloging-in-Publication Data
Haywood, Carolyn, 1898-
Primrose day.
(A Voyager/HBJ book)
Reprint. Originally published: New York : Harcourt, Brace, 1942.
Summary: The adventures of a little English girl who comes to America during World War II to live with her aunt and uncle and her cousin Jerry.
[1. British Americans—Fiction] I. Title.
PZ7.H31496Pr 1986 [Fic] 86-4620
ISBN 0-15-263510-6

Printed in the United States of America

A B C D E

To Cornelia Greenough
my loving critic

CONTENTS

PRIMROSE DAY

CHAPTER 1

MERRY LEAVES FOR AMERICA

MERRY PRIMROSE RAMSAY was almost seven years old. She was named Merry because her mother loved merry little girls and Primrose because she was born in the month of April when the primroses bloom in England.

Merry lived in England in the big city of London. When asked whom she lived with, she would reply, "I live with my mummy and daddy, Greggie and Molly and Annie." Greggie was a Scottie dog whose name was really MacGregor. Molly was a make-believe playmate and Annie was the cook.

When people asked Merry where she lived she would say, "I live at No. 8 Heartford Square." Then everyone knew that Merry lived in a house that faced a little park. Merry was glad she lived in a house on a square. She liked walking past the houses on one side of the square, then across the end of the square and down the other side. The houses were built of red brick and they all had white stone steps. They were very close together. Merry thought they looked like faces with their cheeks touching. The square was a cozy place to live.

But the nicest part about living on the square was the little park. All around the park there was a high iron railing. There was a gate at each end. The people who lived on the square had keys so that they could go in and out of the gates. There were flowerbeds and trees in the park. In the spring there were tulips in the flowerbeds. The paths were covered with pebbles and sometimes Merry would find a very pretty pebble.

Then she would put it in her pocket and carry it home to show to Mummy.

There were benches in the park too. On clear days there were always nurses sitting on the benches. They watched over the little children while they played. All of the nurses were called "Nanny." Merry had had a Nanny when she was little but now that she was almost seven years old, she didn't need a nurse to watch her. She was old enough to take care of herself.

One afternoon, Merry stood at the front window. It was February and it was raining. No one was in the park. The benches were shiny wet. The bare trees dripped. Tiny rivers ran between the pebbles in the paths. Merry pressed her nose against the windowpane. "Do you know what, Molly?" she said to her make-believe playmate. "I'm going to America. I'm going to America to stay with Aunt Helen and Uncle Bill and my cousin Jerry. You see, Molly, it's because of the war. Mummy says when people are selfish and afraid of each other they go to war and hurt each other. All of the boys and girls in my school have gone away from London. Mummy and Daddy are sending me to America until the war is all over. I'm going all by myself too. Daddy can't go because he is doing very important work for the King. And Mummy can't go because England needs her too. So I'm going alone."

Merry turned away from the window and began to set out her doll's tea-set. When Greggie heard the rattle of the dishes, he came into the room. Greggie knew that where there are dishes there may be food. He never missed any if he could help it.

"Greggie, you are going to America, too," said Merry.

Greggie cocked one ear.

"And I'm going to take you too, Molly. Do you think you will like to go to America?"

Just then the front door closed. Merry set a cup on the table and ran to the head of the stairs. Greggie tore along at her heels.

"Daddy!" she called. "Is that you, Daddy?"

"Right you are!" called Daddy.

Merry started down the stairs at a run. Half way down, she stopped still. Daddy stood at the bottom of the stairs. He was wearing a soldier's uniform. Merry hadn't seen her daddy in a soldier's uniform before. He looked strange and different. Merry went down the last six steps very slowly. Her face was grave and her eyes were very big. When she reached the second step, Daddy took her in his arms. "How do you like me, little one?" he asked.

"All right," murmured Merry, "only you don't look like Daddy."

Daddy rubbed his cheek against Merry's. "Do I feel like Daddy?" he asked.

Merry hugged him very tight. "Yes," she said, "you scratch like Daddy." Then they both laughed.

The night before Merry was to leave for America, her mummy packed her bag. She put in all of Merry's winter clothes and all of her summer clothes, her underwear and her stockings. She packed her winter pajamas and her summer nightgowns. On the very top she placed her warm dressing-gown. Her shoes and her bedroom slippers were tucked in the side of the suitcase. Into a little rubber envelope, she put Merry's toothbrush and sponge. Merry sat on the bed and watched her. At last the lid was closed. Merry heard the lock snap shut.

"Mummy," said Merry, "do you think you could sleep in my bed tonight?"

"Yes, darling," said Mummy. "I'll sleep in your bed tonight."

Merry lay in her bed and waited for Mummy. She wondered why it took Mummy so long to get ready for bed. At last she came. She turned out the light beside the bed. Then she lay down beside her little girl. "Oh, Mummy!" cried Merry, "you have lain right on top of Molly!"

"Dear, dear!" said Mummy. "It is so hard for me to know where Molly is. Do you think she will mind very much?"

"Well, if you could lift up a little, she could get out," said Merry.

Mummy lifted up a little. "Now I hope Molly has found a comfortable spot," she said.

Merry snuggled into her mother's arms. "Mummy," she whispered, "do I have to go to America?"

"Yes, dear," replied Mummy.

"But why, Mummy?" asked Merry. "Don't you and Daddy want me here with you?"

"Well, you see, darling, Aunt Helen and Uncle Bill haven't any little girl and Daddy and I want to share our little girl with them."

"But you won't have any little girl while I am in America," said Merry.

"It won't be long, dear," said Mummy. "You will be back almost before I can say 'Jack Robinson.' What a lot you will have to tell Daddy and me."

Merry was quiet a long time. Mummy thought she was asleep but Merry was thinking. After a while she said, "Mummy, I'm not going to take Molly to America with me. I'm going to leave her with you to be your little girl."

"Oh, Merry!" said Mummy, hugging her very tight, "how sweet of you to want to leave Molly with me!"

Merry thought again for a long time. She was having a very hard time deciding something. At last she whispered, "I'll leave Greggie too, if you want him."

"No, dear," replied Mummy, "you must take Greggie with you. I'll be very happy with Molly."

"You'll be very careful not to sit on her or lie on her, won't you?" asked Merry.

"Indeed, I'll be very careful always to notice where she is," replied Mummy.

"That's good," sighed Merry. "I'm really very glad Greggie is going with me." Then she ran her fingers in her mother's soft hair and went to sleep.

The next morning everyone was up very early. Mr. and Mrs. Ramsay were going to take Merry to the boat to go to America.

When Mummy brushed Merry's hair, Merry said,

"Molly has golden curls, you know."

"No, I didn't know that Molly has golden curls," said Mummy. "I'm glad you told me. I'll brush them every day while you are away."

When Merry went downstairs to breakfast, her daddy fastened a little chain around her neck. A metal tag hung from the chain. On one side of the tag was Merry's name, her daddy's name and her address in London. On the other side was the name and address of Merry's Uncle Bill in America. "Now you can't get lost," said Daddy.

Merry sat down at the breakfast table. Beside her plate there was a little box. Merry picked up the box and opened it. There was a tiny golden ring. It had a little blue stone in the center and a pearl on each side. "Oh!" said Merry. "Is it for me?"

"Yes," said Mummy. "It is a remembrance present from Daddy and me."

Merry slipped the ring on her finger. "Oh, thank you," she said; "it's beautiful!"

Merry could hardly eat her breakfast for looking at her new ring. She had never had a ring before.

After breakfast Merry said good-by to Annie, the

cook. "Will you see that Molly has her tea every afternoon, Annie?" said Merry.

"That I will," said Annie. Annie's eyes were red and she wiped a tear on her apron.

"What is the matter, Annie?" asked Merry. "You're crying."

"Oh, 'tis only the onions," she replied. "They always make me cry when I peal them."

"Come, Merry," called Daddy, "the cab is waiting."

Annie pushed a little box into Merry's hand. "There! Gum-drops!" said Annie. "Just a little going-away present for you."

"Oh, thank you, Annie," said Merry.

Annie watched her as she ran down the front steps and jumped into the cab. "She's so little," sobbed Annie, "so little to be going away all by herself."

Merry sat between her mummy and daddy. On her lap she held her best doll, Bonnie. Her suitcase was in front with the driver.

In a moment they were off. When they were half way to the station, Merry suddenly remembered Greggie. "Where's Greggie?" she cried.

"Gracious!" shouted Daddy. "We have forgotten Greggie! I put him in his traveling basket and left him in the kitchen."

Daddy pulled his watch out of his pocket. "We can't

go back now," he said. "If we do, we will miss the boat train."

"Oh, Daddy!" cried Merry; "what will I do without Greggie? What will I do!" Tears ran down Merry's cheeks. Mummy put her arm around her and she leaned her head on Mummy's breast. "Don't cry, my pet," said Mummy. "Don't cry, dear."

"Oh, Mummy! Mummy!" she sobbed. "I don't want to go to America without Greggie. What will he do without me?"

Mummy tried to comfort her little girl but Merry cried all the way to the station.

At the station there were crowds of people. Daddy took Merry's suitcase and hurried Merry and her mummy through the crowd. They had to walk a long way to the train. When they reached it, they climbed into one of the little compartments. Soon they were settled for the long journey to the boat. Merry was still crying.

In a few moments the conductor came past and

slammed the doors.

"Oh, Greggie!" sobbed Merry. "My little Greggie!"

Suddenly there was a shrill toot of the train whistle. The train started with a jolt. Then it stopped. Daddy lowered the window and looked out. What did he see but Annie running down the platform beside the train. She was puffing and panting. In her hand she carried the basket with Greggie inside.

Mr. Ramsay waved to her. "Here we are, Annie," he shouted. "Here we are!"

Just then the train began to move. Annie rushed up to the window. Mr. Ramsay reached out and grabbed the basket.

"I saw the basket the minute you left," she shouted. "I ran to the corner and jumped in a cab."

Daddy and Merry were both leaning out of the window now. "Oh, thank you, Annie," cried Daddy.

"Thank you, thank you, Annie," shouted Merry.

Merry waved to Annie as long as she could see her. Then she settled down between Mummy and Daddy.

She took the basket on her lap and opened it. She patted Greggie's head. Greggie licked her hand. "Oh, Greggie!" said Merry. "I'm so glad you didn't miss the train."

CHAPTER 2

WHAT HAPPENED ON THE LONG TRAIN TRIP

MERRY spent the morning looking out of the window of the train. She liked to watch the pretty English countryside. The plowed fields looked like great big rugs. The train went so fast that the farms, the meadows, the trees, the cows, the sheep—everything, flew past the windows. Sometimes the clouds seemed to race with the train. Station after station flew by. Merry and her daddy made a game of trying to read the names on the stations. Daddy said it was the first time he had ever been on a train without knowing where he was going. No one on the train knew. All they knew was that they were on their way to the boat. The place was a secret.

Merry said, "Why is it a secret, Daddy?"

"Well," said Daddy, "when there is a war everything is a secret."

After a while Merry said, "Mummy, who will take care of me on the boat?"

"There will be nurses to take care of all of the children," replied Mummy. "You will be a very good girl and not make any trouble for the nurses, won't you, dear?"

"Of course I'll be good," said Merry; "but I wish I knew somebody who was going on the boat to America."

"You will soon get to know the other children," said Mummy.

Merry sat swinging her legs and looking at the floor. She was beginning to feel that she didn't want to go to America all by herself.

Suddenly, down on the floor, she saw something that she had never, never seen on a railway train before. She could hardly believe her eyes. There on the floor in the doorway sat a toad. Before Merry could speak, the toad hopped right up on the seat beside Merry.

"Daddy!" she screamed. "There's a toad!" Merry leaped into her daddy's lap.

Just then a little boy appeared in the doorway. "Did you see Jinks?" he asked.

"Donald!" shouted Merry.

"Why, Donald!" cried Mr. and Mrs. Ramsay. They had never been so surprised. Donald was a little American boy. He had been in Merry's class in school and his mother was a friend of Mrs. Ramsay. His father sent all of the news about England to a big American newspaper.

"Hello, Merry!" said Donald. "Did you see my toad? Oh, here he is," he added, picking up the toad. "Hello, Mr. and Mrs. Ramsay! Are you going to America too?"

"No, Donald, Merry is going. Are you going to America?" said Mr. Ramsay.

"Yes, Mr. Ramsay," replied Donald. "Mother and I are both going. You see, we are Americans. We have to go back to America. Only my daddy can stay because he works for the paper."

By this time Mrs. Baker, Donald's mother, had come to look for him. When she saw the Ramsays she was surprised too. Merry was delighted to see her, for she was very fond of Donald's pretty mother.

"Do come sit with us," said Mrs. Ramsay. "I am so glad to see you."

"I'll go get my box for Jinks," said Donald.

Donald ran off to get his box and his mother sat down beside Mrs. Ramsay.

"Oh," said Mrs. Ramsay, "you don't know how much better I feel now that I know that you will be on the boat with Merry." She looked at Merry's daddy and they smiled at each other.

Mrs. Baker put her arm around Merry. "I'm glad too," she said. "It will be so nice to have a little girl with me."

Donald came back with a cardboard box. "Do you want to see my menagerie?" he asked.

Merry sat down beside Donald. She leaned over and watched him take the lid off of the box. The moment the lid was lifted, out jumped the toad again. Donald caught him and held him in his hand. Merry looked into the box. "E-e-e-e-e-e-e-e!" she screamed. "There's a snake in the box!" Merry ran to her daddy.

"He's just a little grass snake," said Donald. "He can't hurt you. His name's Pinkie." Donald picked Pinkie up in his hand and watched him wriggle.

"E-e-e-e-e-e!" squealed Merry. "I don't like snakes." Merry hid her face on Daddy's shoulder.

"O.K.!" said Donald. "I'll put him in my pocket. Gee, girls are funny!"

Donald put Pinkie in his pocket and Merry sat down again. She sat on the side away from the pocket where Pinkie was hidden.

"Well, you're not afraid of turtles, are you?" said Donald. Merry looked into the box again. There lay three little turtles. "No," said Merry. "I like turtles."

"That's Oscar," said Donald, pointing to the largest

turtle. "And that one is Rusty and this one is Pete."

"Are you going to take them to America with you?" asked Merry.

"Sure," said Donald, as he put Jinks, the toad, back into the box.

Most of the people on the train had brought their lunches in boxes. Merry and Donald and Mr. and Mrs. Ramsay and Mrs. Baker ate their lunch together. When they finished, Donald put some crumbs into the box for the toad and the turtles. Then he put his hand in his pocket to get Pinkie. To Donald's great surprise, Pinkie wasn't there. He felt in one pocket. Then he felt in the other. Pinkie wasn't in either pocket.

"Hey, I've lost Pinkie!" cried Donald.

Donald looked all around. "Get up everybody. Get up, please. I've lost Pinkie," he said.

Everyone got up and looked around. All except Merry. She stood on the seat in the corner. She didn't like snakes. Donald got down on his hands and knees and looked under the seats. There was no Pinkie. He felt down in all of the cracks around the seats but he couldn't find his little snake. Then he looked out in the corridor. There was no snake in sight. He felt in his pockets again. "Where do you suppose he got to?" asked Donald.

"I wish you would find him," said Merry. "I don't want him to surprise me again."

Everyone looked around again. Pinkie could not be found. They all settled down and Donald went exploring in the corridor to see if he could find his little snake. Mrs. Baker picked up her knitting-bag from the seat where Donald had been sitting. She took out her knitting. Out popped Pinkie to the floor.

"E-e-e-e-e-e-e!" squealed Merry again.

"Merry, that little snake won't hurt you," said Daddy. "See, it is perfectly harmless." Daddy picked it up. Merry looked at it.

"Just touch it with your finger," said Daddy; "then you won't be afraid of it any longer."

Merry put her finger out very timidly. It wasn't so

bad. It just felt a little rough.

"I'll tell you what," said Daddy, "you take the little snake and give it to Donald. Think how surprised he will be."

Merry looked at Pinkie. She didn't want to do it but it would be fun to surprise Donald, she thought. She picked up the snake in a very gingerly way and went to find Donald. Just outside of the door she met him. "Here's your Pinkie," she said, holding out the snake.

Donald was so surprised he could hardly believe his eyes. "I thought you were a sissy," he said. "I thought you were afraid of a little grass snake."

"Well, I'm not now," said Merry.

When she sat down beside Daddy, he put his arm around her. "Good girl!" he whispered.

By the end of the day they reached the sea. When the train finally stopped, Merry said, "Is this where I get on the boat?"

"No," said Daddy, "but this is where we will hand you over to the nurses. They will take you to the boat. This is as far as Mummy and I can go with you."

Merry held very tightly to Mummy's and Daddy's hands. The time had come to say "Good-by." There was a big lump in her throat. She couldn't swallow. "Mummy," she whispered, "I don't want to go."

"Oh, come now!" said Mummy. "Don't forget that you are Mummy's merry little girl. Aunt Helen and Uncle Bill and Jerry are waiting for you. They would be so disappointed if you didn't come. They will be waiting for you in New York when you get there."

Merry felt surrounded with people now. Everyone had gotten off of the train. There were grown-ups and children. Merry thought she had never seen so many children. Daddy went into an office to sign some papers. Donald and his mother went off too.

Mr. Ramsay came back alone. "We have to put her on this other train," he said.

"Where are Donald and Mrs. Baker?" asked Merry.

"They will meet you at the train," replied Daddy.

Merry walked between her mummy and daddy to the train. There they met the nurse who was to take care of Merry. Her name was Miss Martin. Merry liked Miss Martin right away because her eyes twinkled when she laughed.

Mummy and Daddy put Merry into the train. They put Greggie's basket on the seat beside her. "Now see that you don't leave Greggie on the train," said Daddy.

Daddy lifted Merry up in his arms and kissed her.

"Good-by, little one," he said. "Be a good girl and write to your daddy." Then Mummy took her little girl in her arms. "Good-by, my darling," said Mummy.

"Good-by, Mummy," whispered Merry, hugging her very tight. "Good-by."

Mummy and Daddy got out of the train and stood on the platform.

Just then Donald rushed up to Mr. Ramsay. "Mr. Ramsay," he said, "they won't let me take my menagerie with me. Will you take them, Mr. Ramsay? Will you take them back to London and give them to my daddy?"

"Sure," said Mr. Ramsay, "but I hope they won't wander all over the train on the way home."

Donald handed the box to Mr. Ramsay and climbed into the train with his mother and Merry. Finally everyone was settled. Merry bit her lip and winked back the tears. She didn't want to cry in front of Donald. He would think she was a baby.

Merry looked out of the window. She could see

Daddy, so tall and straight. He had his arm around Mummy. They both waved their handkerchiefs. Merry waved hers. The train pulled out. They were off.

It was dark now. All of the shades were pulled down to keep the light from shining out of the windows. In about an hour they stopped. Everyone got out of the train. Mrs. Baker took hold of the two children's hands. They walked a long way. It was so dark Merry couldn't see very much. In a few moments she could see that they were going up a narrow boardwalk. They were going up to a high deck on the biggest boat that Merry had ever seen. Merry didn't know that boats could be so big. When she reached the deck, she was surprised to find that it was as wide as the library at home.

The children had to go right to bed. Merry had a tiny cabin. It had two berths in it. She was sorry it was so far away from Mrs. Baker and Donald. They were at the other end of the boat. Merry got undressed and climbed into her berth. She began to feel very lonely.

She wished that Greggie was with her. But Greggie had to stay in a kennel down in the bottom of the boat. She hoped Greggie wouldn't cry for her. The big lump came up in her throat again. She held her doll, Bonnie, very tight. It seemed so strange not to have Mummy tuck her in and kiss her good night.

Just then the door opened and a little girl came into the cabin. Merry heard Miss Martin say, "Get undressed and I will be back in a few minutes."

Merry looked at the little girl. She was the prettiest little girl Merry had ever seen. She had golden curls that hung around her shoulders and dimples in her cheeks. She was the only little girl Merry had ever seen who looked just like her make-believe playmate, Molly.

"Hello," said Merry.

"Hello," said the little girl. "What's your name?"

"Merry," said Merry.

"That's a pretty name," said the little girl. "My name is Molly."

Merry could hardly believe her ears. Her eyes were

like saucers. Miss Martin opened the door. She was carrying two bowls of hot milk and crackers. "Well," she said, "how are you two getting along?"

"Fine," said Merry. "Miss Martin, what do you think?"

"I haven't an idea," said Miss Martin.

"Well," said Merry, "I left my make-believe playmate, Molly, home with Mummy so that she would have a little girl."

"You did?" said Miss Martin.

"Yes," said Merry, "and what do you think?"

"What?" said Miss Martin.

"Why, now I have a Molly too!" said Merry.

CHAPTER 3

A REMEMBRANCE PRESENT FOR MOLLY

MERRY and Donald and Molly soon felt at home on the big boat. There were so many things to do and so many places to explore.

At night when Molly and Merry lay in their berths they told each other stories and ate the gum-drops that

Annie had given Merry. Merry loved Molly very much indeed and Molly thought that Merry was the nicest little girl she had ever known.

Every morning after breakfast Merry would go down to the kennels and get Greggie. Greggie was al-

ways looking for her. He knew as soon as he saw her that he was going for a walk. After lunch Merry would take him for another walk. She wished that she could have Greggie in her cabin so that she and Molly could play with him but that was against the rules. Dogs were not allowed in the cabins. So after each walk Greggie would have to go back to his kennel. Merry would pat him on the head and say, "Never mind, Greggie, we'll soon be to America."

Day after day the boat moved slowly through thick fog. It was like being in a cloud. Sometimes when the children looked over the railing around the boat they could hardly see the ocean.

At first Merry wished that the sun would shine so that the boat could go faster. Soon she was glad they were going slowly. It was such fun to be with her new friend, Molly.

One night, after the little girls were in bed, Merry said, "Molly, where are you going to live in America?"

"I'm going to live with Mr. and Mrs. Price," said

Molly. "They are friends of Mummy's."

"But where do they live?" asked Merry.

"I forget the name of the place," said Molly; "but it is all written down on my papers."

"I'm going to live with my Aunt Helen and Uncle Bill," said Merry. "They live at Rose Valley."

"Oh, do you think it is full of roses?" asked Molly.

"I guess so," said Merry. "I hope it is full of primroses, too."

"I wish I were going to live at Rose Valley," said Molly.

"I wish so too," replied Merry.

In a few minutes Merry said, "Do you like to pick primroses, Molly?"

There was no answer. Molly was sound asleep.

Merry lay looking into the thick darkness. She was thinking of Molly. She wished that she had something that she could give Molly for a remembrance present, like the little ring that Mummy and Daddy had given her. Merry tried to think of something she could give

Molly. She couldn't think of anything. She wished that she had brought the bag of blue beads that she had left in her desk drawer. She could have made Molly a necklace. She thought a necklace would be the nicest thing she could give her. How she wished that she had brought the beads.

She thought of everything she had with her. Suddenly she thought of the box of gum-drops. She snapped on the little bedlight. Then she hung down over the side of her berth. She reached under and pulled out the gum-drop box. She took off the lid. The gum-drops were nearly all gone. There were two big green ones and one smaller white one. Merry was glad to see that there were three gum-drops left. She would make Molly a gum-drop man. She would ask Harry, the waiter in the dining room, for some raisins to make the arms and the legs.

Merry snapped the light off and went to sleep.

The next morning she ate her breakfast very slowly. Molly and Donald were finished a long time ahead of

Merry.

"Hurry up, slowpoke!" cried Donald.

"Oh, Merry!" said Molly. "You're not half through your porridge!"

"Don't let's wait for her," said Donald. "She's too poky."

"I don't mind if you want to go," said Merry.

"We'll see you up on deck," said Donald, as he got down off his chair.

"Don't be too long," said Molly, and she ran after Donald.

Merry was alone now and that was just what she wanted. She finished her porridge and Harry brought her a soft-boiled egg.

"Harry," said Merry, "could I have some raisins?"

"Raisins!" exclaimed Harry. "I never heard of eating raisins with eggs."

"I don't want to eat them," said Merry. "I want to make arms and legs on a gum-drop man. It's going to be a remember present for Molly."

"I see," said Harry. "And I suppose you want some toothpicks, too?"

"Yes," said Merry, "and something to make a face."

"Well, I'll see what I can do," said Harry as he went off to the kitchen.

Just as Merry finished her egg, Harry returned. Wrapped in a paper napkin were six toothpicks, some raisins, and a few cloves.

"Here you are," said Harry.

"Oh, thank you!" said Merry. "If I had some more gum-drops I would make one for you, Harry."

"That's kind of you," said Harry. "I would like to see it when it is finished."

Merry trotted off with her package. She went right to her cabin and locked the door. She sat on the floor and pulled the box of gum-drops from under her berth. She put a toothpick through the two green gum-drops. Then she fastened the white one on top of the green ones. She stuck four cloves into the white one. These made the nose, the eyes, and the mouth. It took a long time to make the arms and legs. Merry put the raisins on the toothpicks very carefully.

She hadn't quite finished one arm when she heard Donald and Molly. They were outside the door. One of the children turned the knob but the door was locked. Then they knocked on the door. Merry sat as still as a mouse.

"Hey, Merry!" called Donald. "Are you in there?"

Merry didn't answer.

"Merry!" called Molly. "Open the door!"

Merry sat so still she hardly breathed.

"Where do you suppose she is?" said Donald.

"I don't know," answered Molly, "but it's awfully funny that the door is locked. It was never locked before."

"Maybe she's down with Greggie," said Donald.

"Well, let's go see," said Molly.

Merry heard the children's footsteps go down the corridor. She let out the breath that she had been holding and went on with the gum-drop man.

When he was finished, he looked very nice indeed. He wore a raisin on his head for a hat. Merry wrapped him in the paper napkin and laid him in the gum-drop box. Then she carried it down to the dining room to show to Harry. "Do you think it is nice, Harry?" asked Merry.

"He's the finest gum-drop man I ever saw," replied Harry.

"Do you think it is nice enough for a remember present?" said Merry.

"Sure, what could be better?" asked Harry.

"Only a necklace," said Merry, "but I left my bag of beads at home. They were nice blue ones too."

"Well, don't worry," said Harry. "The gum-drop man is a fine present."

Merry went back to her cabin, pleased with her gum-drop man. She stowed the box away under her berth. She had decided not to give it to Molly until they reached America.

Several days later, Merry was taking Greggie for a walk around the deck. In a few moments she saw Donald running towards her. "Hey, Merry!" he shouted. "The Captain is going to take Molly and me up on the bridge. You got to come right away if you want to go up; but you can't bring Greggie with you."

"Will you wait until I put him in his kennel?" asked

Merry.

"No, we can't wait that long," said Donald.

"But what will I do with him?"

"Put him in your cabin," said Donald.

"But he isn't allowed in the cabin," replied Merry.

"Aw, he'll be all right for a little while," said Donald. "Hurry up!"

Merry picked up Greggie and ran inside to her cabin. She pushed the little dog through the door and closed it. Then she ran to join the Captain and the other children.

It was such fun to be on the bridge. Merry had looked up at it many times. There was always an officer on the bridge. The Captain showed the children the instruments that were used to guide the boat. Donald said that he was going to be a captain of a boat when he grew up.

After the children came down from the bridge, they decided to play hide-and-seek.

Merry forgot all about Greggie. She never thought

of him until she went to her cabin to wash her hands for supper. When she opened the door, Greggie jumped up to greet her.

"Oh, Greggie!" cried Merry. "What have you done!"

All over the cabin floor there were pieces of paper and cardboard. Here and there were raisins. The toothpicks that had held the gum-drop man together were scattered under the berth. The gum-drops were gone.

"Oh, Greggie!" cried Merry. "You've eaten my gum-drop man! You've eaten my present for Molly!"

Just then Miss Martin appeared. Merry told her what had happened. It was hard for Merry to keep back the tears.

"Well," said Miss Martin, "you shouldn't have put Greggie in here. You know that it is against the rules."

"Yes, I know," said Merry. "I knew it was wrong when I did it. Now I haven't any present for Molly."

Merry took Greggie down to his kennel. She felt

very sad. After dinner she told Harry about the awful thing that had happened to the gum-drop man.

"Tut, tut!" said Harry. "And he was such a nice gum-drop man! Well, never mind. Maybe you will find something else for a present for Molly."

"I don't think so," said Merry very sadly. "I wish I had brought my beads."

The next morning when Merry met the Captain, he said, "Well, Merry, we reach America tomorrow."

Only one more day and Merry would be in New York with Aunt Helen and Uncle Bill and Jerry. She would have to think fast if she was going to give Molly a remembrance present.

That day there was macaroni for lunch. As Merry ate the little white elbows of macaroni she suddenly had an idea. She slowed down. By the time Donald and Molly were ready for their dessert, Merry was still eating macaroni.

"Don't wait for me," said Merry, "eat your dessert."

"Gee! You're slow, Merry," said Donald.

When Donald and Molly finished, Donald said, "Come on, Molly. Merry's too slow."

"No," said Molly, "I'm going to wait for Merry."

"But I don't want you to wait for me," said Merry.

"But I want to wait for you," said Molly.

"Well, I'm going to be an awfully, awfully long time," said Merry.

"I don't mind," replied Molly; "I'll wait for you."

"Well, I'm going," said Donald, and he ran off.

Harry had been listening. In a few minutes he leaned over and said to Molly, "I think they are giving out American flags up on deck. You had better hurry if you want one."

"Oh!" said Molly. "I'll run up and get one and I'll get one for you too, Merry."

Molly ran off.

"Now," said Harry to Merry, "and what do you want? More raisins?"

"No," answered Merry, "macaroni."

"Macaroni!" gasped Harry. "Why, you haven't

eaten all that is on your plate."

"I want some that isn't cooked," said Merry. "And I want a piece of string. I'm going to make Molly a necklace after all."

Merry gave Molly her necklace just before the boat landed at New York. Molly thought it was a beautiful necklace. She said that she had never seen one made of macaroni before.

"I guess not," said Merry. "I guess maybe it is the only macaroni necklace in the whole world."

CHAPTER 4

JERRY GOES TO MEET THE BOAT

JERRY's name was really Jeremy Hobson but everyone called him Jerry. He was seven years old. His mother was Mrs. Ramsay's sister. Jerry had been to England with his mother and father when he was five years old. They had stayed with the Ramsays in Heartford Square and Jerry and Merry had played together in the little park. They had been happy days.

Jerry was delighted when he heard that Merry was coming to stay with them. He hadn't any brothers or sisters. Now he would have a playmate who lived right in his own house.

The Hobsons lived in the country about fifteen miles away from a big city. They lived in a white house that stood on the edge of a little woods. There was a garden behind the house and a place to play croquet. In front of the house there were two apple trees. These were nice for climbing. In the spring they were covered with blossoms and in the fall with bright red apples. Jerry's father had fastened a bird-feeding platform on one of the trees. There Jerry put crumbs and seeds and little pieces of suet.

A bright yellow bus took Jerry to school in the mornings and brought him home in the afternoons. At half-past eight in the morning Jerry would run to the corner of the street. There he would wait for the bus. In a few minutes it would come rattling along.

"Hi! Jerry!" the children would shout, as Jerry

climbed into the bus.

One morning when the bus stopped, Jerry didn't climb in. Instead, he ran up to the driver and called, "I'm not going this morning, Mr. Jones. My cousin is coming from England and we're going to New York to meet the boat. We just got the telegram."

"O.K.," said Mr. Jones. "See you tomorrow."

Jerry ran back to the house. Father was opening the garage doors. Mother was already in the car.

"Hurry up, Jerry. Hop in," said Father. "We haven't much time to make the train."

Jerry jumped into the back of the car and Father climbed into the front seat. He put his hand in his pocket to get his keys. They were not there. Then he felt in his other pocket. The keys were not there either. "Where are my keys?" he muttered.

"Here," said Mother, opening her handbag. "Use mine."

Mother poked around in her handbag. She couldn't find her keys anywhere. "Oh!" she cried, "now I remember. I left my keys in my other bag."

"Good gracious!" said Father. "Haven't you a door key either?"

"No," replied Mother. "Haven't you a door key?"

"No," said Father. "All of my keys are in the pocket of my brown suit."

Mother and Father just looked at each other.

"What will we do?" said Jerry.

"I locked every window in the house," said Father.

"Oh, dear!" said Mother. "If only Sarah were here!" Sarah was the maid. She had gone off the night before to spend the night with her sister. "She won't be back before eleven o'clock," said Mother as she got out of the car.

"Well, the boat docks at noon in New York," said Father. He tried all of the windows. He couldn't budge them.

"I tell you, Jerry," he said. "Maybe you can get in through the little bathroom window. It may not be locked. Here, climb up the apple tree."

Father boosted Jerry up into the apple tree. Jerry went from limb to limb until he reached the roof under the bathroom window. He stepped on the roof and walked over to the window. He tried to push up the sash. He couldn't move it. "It's locked too," he shouted.

"Jumping juniper!" cried Father. "We've got to get that next train. It connects with the nine-thirty to New York. We have to make the nine-thirty."

"Oh, dear!" said Mother. "Try your window, Jerry."

"It's no use," said Father. "I remember I locked it."

Jerry went over to his window. Suddenly the window flew up and Sarah stuck her head out.

"Sakes alive!" she cried; "what are you doing on the roof?"

"Lemme in," said Jerry, climbing over the sill.

"Sarah," shouted Mrs. Hobson, "where did you come from?"

"I came up through the woods and in the back door," said Sarah. "I just read your note saying you had gone to New York."

"Mr. Hobson and I both left our keys inside the house," said Mrs. Hobson.

"Good thing I came back early," said Sarah.

By this time Jerry was down with the keys.

Father took them and they all climbed into the car. Then they heard the shrill toot of a train whistle.

"That's the train," said Father, as he backed the car out of the garage. "We will never get to the station in time to make it."

"Maybe we can catch it at the next station if we cut across country," said Mother.

Father stepped on the gas and the car flew ahead. Very soon they could see the station. "Do you think we have missed it?" said Jerry.

"No," said Father. "I can see the people waiting on the platform. If that traffic light ahead doesn't change, we can make it."

"Toot! Toot!" the whistle sounded. The train wasn't very far away. Jerry sat on the edge of the seat. He stared at the green light. "Stay green," he said to himself, "stay green, stay green."

Jerry's heart sank. The light turned white and then red. Father jammed on the brakes and the car stopped. While they waited for the light to change, the train pulled into the station. They watched the people get on the train. Father blew his horn as loud as he could. He hoped the conductor would hear it and hold the train. But the conductor didn't hear it. Just as the light turned green, the train pulled out of the station.

"We have got to catch that train," said Father.

"Do you think we can get it at the next station?" asked Jerry.

"Well, here goes!" said Father.

He turned down the road that led to the next station. The car flew along. In a few minutes they could see the station.

"Has it come yet?" gasped Jerry.

"Not yet," said Mother. "I can see people waiting."

This time there wasn't any traffic light. Father

swung the car into the station driveway just as the train arrived. He drove up beside the parked cars and pulled on the brake. Jerry jumped out of the car and ran toward the train. He shouted, "Wait, conductor! Please wait for my mother and father."

"I'll wait," said the conductor, "don't worry." The conductor pushed Jerry up the steps and held the train for his father and mother. They were all out of breath. "Whe-e-e-e-e!" said Father. "What a race!"

"That was great," said Jerry, "but my knees are shaky."

"Well," said Father, "we made it, anyway. Now we don't have anything to worry about. We have eight minutes between this train and the New York train. Jerry will even have time to buy a bar of chocolate."

Father opened up his morning paper and Mother took out her knitting. Jerry looked out of the window. There was one place, on the way to the city, where there were cows. Jerry always watched for them.

Suddenly there was a screech of brakes. The train

stopped so suddenly that Jerry fell right off of the seat.

"Now what!" said Father.

Jerry scrambled back into his seat. "Is it a train wreck?" he asked.

"No," said Mother, "it isn't a train wreck."

The people in the train began to open the windows and stick their heads out. "Can't see a thing," they said to each other.

Father got up and walked to the door. He went down the steps. The conductor came running along beside the train. "What's up?" said Mr. Hobson.

"Well, believe it or not, there's a cow on the track," said the conductor. "She's lying right down on the track."

"Well, can't you get her up?" asked Mr. Hobson.

"Can't budge her," answered the conductor.

Mr. Hobson went back into the train. "Anybody know how to get a cow off the track?" he called out.

Everyone on the train laughed. Several men got up and walked to the door. Mr. Hobson and the men walked to the front of the train. Sure enough, there was a big cow, lying on the track and calmly chewing her cud. The engineer was trying to coax her off the track. She seemed to like it where she was. She didn't intend to move.

Just as Jerry joined his father, the conductor said, "Guess we'll have to shove her off."

The men got together and tried to shove the cow off the track. She just rolled over. Things were as bad as before.

Then a little old lady got off the train. She had a market basket on her arm. She trotted up to the group of men. "Here," she said, "I'll get that cow off the track."

The men looked at the old lady in surprise. They watched her as she reached into her basket. She pulled out a package of salt. She emptied some into her hand and went over to the cow. She held her hand near the cow's mouth. The cow stuck out her tongue and licked the salt. Then the old lady held her hand higher and the cow got up. The old lady walked slowly away from the train track and the cow followed. She kept licking the old lady's hand. When she was a safe distance from the train, the old lady left the cow. Everyone climbed back into the train. Mr. Hobson carried the old lady's market basket. She chuckled to herself. "I've been up to market early this morning," she said. "It's a good thing I'd run out of salt."

"It certainly is," said Mr. Hobson.

"Do you think we will make the train to New York, Father?" said Jerry.

"Well," said Father, "we lost ten minutes but we may make some of it up."

When they reached the big city terminal, they had one minute to make the train. Father took hold of Jerry's hand and they all ran. Just as they ran through the gate, the conductor shouted, "All aboard!"

Mother and Father and Jerry climbed the steps. By the time they found three seats the train was going at full speed.

"Well," said Jerry, as he settled down, "I hope we don't meet any more cows. Do you think the boat will be on time, Father?"

"It's due at noon," said Father. "I telegraphed ahead for passes so that we can go out on the pier."

Jerry looked out of the window. The train crossed two rivers and it stopped at three stations. After what seemed a long time the train shot into a long dark tunnel. "Now we are in the Hudson Tunnel," said Father.

Jerry knew then that the train was going under the Hudson River. It was hard to believe that deep water was above his head.

In a few moments the train reached the station. Everyone got out. The platform was crowded with people and baggage and porters.

Father took Mother and Jerry to the taxi-stand. They got into a taxicab and the cab started for the pier. Jerry felt excited as they sped up the wide New York streets. Everything looked so big. The first stop was in front of a great big building. It was the Customs House. Here Father got the passes to go on the pier. Jerry and Mother waited for him in the taxicab.

It was just ten minutes of twelve when they reached the pier. Father paid the taxi driver. Then he went into an office to see if the boat was on time. Mother and Jerry waited by the elevator. When he returned, he said, "The boat is just coming in."

When they got off the elevator, Jerry found that he was on a great big pier.

"I wonder if we shall know Merry when we see her," said Mother.

"Well, I'll know Greggie if I don't know Merry," said Jerry. "I used to have fun with Greggie. I'm glad Merry is bringing him with her."

They were almost out to the end of the pier now. There were a great many people. They were all looking up at the big boat. The boat was getting nearer and nearer the pier.

All of the people on the boat were hanging over the

railings around the decks. It was hard to tell them apart. There seemed to be a great many children. Everyone was waving. Some waved their handkerchiefs and some waved little American flags.

Jerry's mother and father strained their eyes, hoping to see Merry. They looked over each deck. They didn't seem to see anyone who looked as they thought Merry would look.

Now the boat was fastened to the pier. In a few minutes the gang-planks were let down. Everyone on the pier crowded around the gang-planks. The people began to come off the boat.

"I bet I'll see her first," said Jerry. "I bet I will."

Jerry was jumping up and down, he was so excited.

People were pouring off the boat now. They shouted to each other. Everyone sounded happy. But there didn't seem to be any little girl who looked as though she were Merry.

Jerry and his mother and father watched and waited. After a long time, a pretty woman appeared

at the top of the gang-plank. She had a little boy by one hand and a little girl by the other. The little girl had a Scottie dog on a leash. He was tugging very hard. The little girl's eyes looked as round as saucers.

"There's Merry!" shouted Jerry. "There she is! There's Greggie too! Didn't I tell you I would know Greggie?"

Jerry ran towards the gang-plank. His father and mother followed. When Merry reached the bottom of the gang-plank, Jerry cried, "Hello, Merry! Hello!"

"Hello, Merry, here's your Uncle Bill," cried Mr. Hobson.

"Merry, Merry darling!" cried Jerry's mother.

"Oh, Aunt Helen!" cried Merry and she ran into Aunt Helen's arms. "It's a long way to America, Aunt Helen! It's a long way!"

CHAPTER 5

MERRY GOES TO SCHOOL

WHEN Merry reached Rose Valley she thought it was a beautiful place. She had never lived in the country. But her mother had taken her on picnics in the country. She had always gone to the country on her birthday to pick primroses. They called it "Merry's Primrose Day."

Merry loved Aunt Helen's house and especially the

little bedroom that Aunt Helen had fixed for her. She was so surprised to find that the curtains at the windows were just like the curtains in her own room at home. They were white with bright red strawberries sprinkled all over them.

"Why, Aunt Helen," said Merry, "these curtains are just like the curtains in my room at home."

"Well now, what do you think of that!" said Aunt Helen. Aunt Helen and Uncle Bill looked at each other and laughed.

"Mother did it on purpose," said Jerry, "so you would feel at home."

"Oh, Jerry," laughed his mother, "you shouldn't have told. That was supposed to be a secret."

"Well, you did," said Jerry. "I heard you say so to Daddy."

"It's a pretty room," said Merry. "I'm going to like living here."

"I am sure you will," said Aunt Helen. "Tomorrow you will start to school. I am going to drive you and

Jerry over to school in the morning. After that you will go in the bus with Jerry."

"Will I be in the same room with Jerry?" asked Merry.

"I suppose so," said Aunt Helen. "Jerry is in the second grade."

"Second grade?" said Merry. "What is grade?"

"It means second year," said Aunt Helen. "You call it second form in England, don't you?"

"Oh, yes!" said Merry. "I was in second form in England."

The following morning Mrs. Hobson drove Merry and Jerry to school. The Principal said that she would try Merry in the second grade.

Jerry took Merry into his room. He walked up to his teacher, Miss Miller.

"Good morning, Jerry," said Miss Miller.

"Good morning, Miss Miller," said Jerry. "This is my cousin, Merry Ramsay. She is from England, you know."

"Good morning, Merry," said Miss Miller, shaking hands with Merry. "Jerry has been telling us that you were coming for a visit. We will be glad to have you in our class."

The boys and girls in the room were all chattering like magpies. Miss Miller clapped her hands. The chatter ceased. "Boys and girls," said Miss Miller, "this is Merry Ramsay from England. Will you all say 'Good morning' to Merry?"

"Good morning, Merry," the children said.

"Good morning," said Merry.

Miss Miller showed Merry to a seat right behind Jerry's.

Soon the bell rang for school to begin. The children sang a song that Merry knew. Then they had a reading lesson. Merry read very well. After the reading lesson the children wrote words on a piece of paper. Merry got them all right. She was beginning to feel that school in America wasn't very different from school in England.

After Miss Miller marked all of the children's papers, she said, "Now, boys and girls, we are going to do some examples on the blackboard."

"Examples!" thought Merry. "What are examples?"

Miss Miller looked at Merry. "I am going to ask our little girl from England to come up to the blackboard," she said.

Merry walked up to the blackboard. She wondered what she was going to do.

"Now," said Miss Miller, "will you write the example, 'ten take away six.' "

Merry picked up a piece of chalk and began to write out the words, "Ten take—"

All of the children began to laugh.

"No, no, Merry," said Miss Miller. "I want you to write the example."

Merry looked puzzled. "I don't know what you mean by 'example,' " she said.

"Golly," said Bobby Brown, "she's dumb!"

"Bobby," said Miss Miller, "that is very rude. It is

te

very rude to laugh too."

Merry bit her lip. She didn't like being laughed at.

"Never mind, Merry," said Miss Miller. "Jerry will write it on the board. Then you will see what I mean."

Jerry went to the front of the room and wrote a big number ten. Underneath it he put a take away sign and the figure six. Then he drew a line under the six and made the figure four.

"Oh!" said Merry, "I didn't know that you wanted me to write a sum."

"Oh, Merry," said Miss Miller, "I am so sorry. I didn't know that you called them 'sums' in England. You see we call them 'examples.' "

"I see," said Merry.

Then Miss Miller told her to write the example, eight take away three. This time Merry knew just what to do.

At recess time Jerry and Merry went out to play.

Bobby Brown came running up to Merry. "Hello, English!" he cried. "How are your sums?"

Merry's cheeks began to feel hot.

Just then Tommy and Freddy Clark rushed up. They were twins and they were always into mischief. They began to call, "Oh, Merry sums! Oh, Merry sums! How are your sums today?"

Merry felt hot tears in her eyes.

"You leave her alone," said Jerry.

The boys ran off shouting, "Merry, Merry sums! Merry, Merry sums!"

When Merry got home from school, she didn't feel very happy. When Aunt Helen asked her how she liked school, she said, "Oh, all right. Only I didn't know that they called 'sums' 'examples.' "

That night, after Aunt Helen had tucked her into bed and closed the door, Merry cried. She felt strange and lonely. She wished she could be with Molly. Molly talked the way she did. Merry buried her face in the pillow and cried until she fell asleep.

The next morning while Merry dressed for school, she was thinking. She wished she didn't have to go to

school. It was so awful to be different from the other children. It was terrible to be laughed at.

After breakfast Aunt Helen said, "This morning you are going on the bus to school."

At half-past eight Jerry and Merry were at the corner, waiting for the bus.

Soon the yellow bus arrived. Jerry and Merry climbed in.

"Hi, Jerry!" the children shouted.

"Hello, English!" cried Bobby.

Merry didn't mind so much being called "English." She was proud to be English. She just hoped he wouldn't say anything about sums. She would remember today to call them examples.

Merry sat down beside Nancy Barnes. Merry liked Nancy. She was a very quiet little girl.

Just before they reached the school a big truck passed the bus. "My!" cried Merry. "What a big lorry!"

"Big what?" said Bobby.

"Big lorry," said Merry.

"That's not a lorry," cried Bobby; "that's a truck."

The children in the bus laughed when Bobby cried out, "She calls a truck a lorry." But Nancy didn't laugh.

Merry felt her cheeks grow hot again. She had made another mistake. At recess time the boys shouted, "Hi, Lorry! Hi, Lorry!" They called her "Lorry" all day.

As the days went by Merry grew more and more unhappy. She was always using words that made the children laugh. Merry would bite her lip to keep back the tears. Aunt Helen said that she mustn't mind. She said that the children didn't mean to be unkind. "They just don't know any better," said Aunt Helen.

One day Miss Miller told the children that she wanted each one to think of the happiest day he could remember. Then she asked several of the children to tell the others the story of their happiest day.

Merry was so anxious to tell about her happiest day that she forgot how the boys had laughed at her. She raised her hand.

"Merry has a story to tell us," said Miss Miller.

Merry walked to the front of the room. She faced the class.

"When I lived in England," she began, "on my birthday every year Mummy took me to the country to pick primroses. We would go on the tram to the railway station."

"On the what?" asked Bobby.

"On the tram," said Merry.

"Bobby, it is rude to interrupt," said Miss Miller. "Merry means that she went on a street-car."

Merry saw a grin spread over Bobby's face. "Oh, dear!" thought Merry. "Now they will laugh at me because I called it a tram."

She went on with the story. "At the railway station," she said, "we got on a train that went down to Devon. Mummy always took a tea-basket so that we could have lunch and tea out of doors. All the way there were primroses growing beside the railway tracks. It looked like a yellow carpet. When we got off the train, Mummy and I would walk a long way. We gathered the primroses from the hedgerows and put them in a basket. Then we would find a lovely place in the woods and eat our lunch. But the most fun was after lunch. After lunch I made primrose chains. I always made one for Mummy and one for me. Mummy and I always called my birthday Merry Primrose Day 'cause my middle name is Primrose."

Nancy raised her hand.

"Nancy wants to ask a question," said Miss Miller. "What is it, Nancy?"

"What is a primrose chain?" asked Nancy.

"Oh, they are pretty," said Merry. "You make a little slit in the stem of one primrose and then you pull the stem of another primrose through the slit. You can make a long chain."

"Now, finish your story, Merry," said Miss Miller.

"Well, there isn't very much more," said Merry. "After tea we took the train back to London and showed our primrose chains to Daddy."

"That was a very nice story," said Miss Miller.

"It won't be long before my birthday," said Merry. "Only this year Aunt Helen will take me to gather primroses."

"I am afraid you will not be able to gather primroses this year," said Miss Miller. "You see, Merry, primroses don't grow in the fields and woods of America."

Merry looked puzzled. "You mean that there are no primroses in America?" said Merry.

"There are a few," said Miss Miller, "but they grow in gardens."

"You mean that you can't go out in the woods and gather them?" asked Merry.

"That's right," said Miss Miller. "You can't go out and gather primroses in America."

Merry sat down at her desk. She couldn't believe that there wouldn't be any primroses on her birthday. Why, as long as she could remember she had always gathered primroses on her birthday. It would be like Christmas without a stocking or a Christmas tree.

On the way home in the bus Merry was so busy feeling sorry about the primroses that she hardly heard Bobby call out, "Hello, English, are you going on a tram?"

When Merry reached home, she rushed into the house and right up the stairs. She threw herself on her bed and cried.

In a few minutes Aunt Helen came into the room. She sat down on Merry's bed. "Merry dear," she said, "what is the matter?"

"There aren't any primroses," sobbed Merry. "I can't pick primroses on my birthday."

"Never mind, darling," said Aunt Helen. "There will be other flowers to pick. I'll take you to pick violets."

"But it won't be the same," cried Merry. "Oh, I wish I were back in England where there are primroses. I wish I were home where people talk the way I do. No-

body laughs at me in England."

Aunt Helen patted Merry's shoulder. "Merry," she said, "there is someone downstairs to see you."

Merry went right on crying.

"It is someone you are very fond of," said Aunt Helen.

Merry turned over and looked at Aunt Helen. "Who is it?" she asked.

"Come and wash your face," said Aunt Helen; "then come downstairs."

Merry got up. She washed her face and brushed her hair. Then she went downstairs. She could hear voices in the library. They were grown-ups. Merry wondered who they were.

When she reached the foot of the stairs, Molly came running out of the library. "Hello, Merry!" she shouted. "Hello! I've come to live in Rose Valley too!"

CHAPTER 6

PRIMROSE DAY

MERRY was so glad to be with Molly again. Mr. and Mrs. Price had moved from the city to Rose Valley. They had taken a house about a half mile from the Hobsons.

When Molly started to school, she was placed in the same room with Merry. Both of the little girls were delighted. With two little English girls in the class the other children soon grew used to the way they spoke. Even Bobby Brown stopped making fun of them.

When Merry told Molly that there were no primroses in America, Molly thought it was very strange. "My birthday won't be a Primrose Day this year," said Merry. "It won't seem like a birthday at all."

Merry's birthday was on the twelfth of April. It fell on a Saturday. The night before, when Aunt Helen tucked her into bed she said, "Merry, tomorrow you and I are going on a picnic."

"All by ourselves?" said Merry.

"Yes, all by ourselves. Just as you did with Mummy," said Aunt Helen.

"Will we take a tea-basket?" asked Merry.

"Yes," replied Aunt Helen, "we'll take a tea-basket. Only we call it a picnic basket."

"And will we stay for lunch and tea?" asked Merry.

"Just for lunch," said Aunt Helen. "We are not going as far away as you used to go with Mummy. We'll come home in time for tea."

"Do you think there will be any flowers to pick?" asked Merry.

"I think so," replied Aunt Helen.

"Maybe there will be violets," said Merry; "but I do wish there were primroses."

"Well, go to sleep," said Aunt Helen, as she kissed Merry good night. "Maybe you will dream that you are picking primroses."

The next morning Merry was up bright and early. It was a beautiful spring day. Merry looked out of the window. There was a big fat robin on the lawn. The apple trees were covered with pale pink blossoms.

When Uncle Bill came down to breakfast, he said, "Happy birthday, Merry."

"Thank you," said Merry. "Daddy always said 'Merry Primrose' on my birthday. Daddy said, 'If you say "Merry Christmas" on Christmas, you should say "Merry Primrose" on my birthday.' "

"I think your daddy is right," said Uncle Bill. "So, Merry Primrose to you."

Just then Aunt Helen came downstairs. She had a birthday letter from Merry's daddy and one from her mummy. There was a photograph of Daddy in one

and one of Mummy in the other. Mummy said that she had asked Aunt Helen to buy her a bottle of perfume for Merry's Primrose Day. Daddy said that he

had asked Aunt Helen to buy her a new hair-ribbon. He said it must be plaid because he was a Scotchman. Merry laughed because Daddy said he hoped that Aunt Helen had taken Greggie with her to buy the ribbon. He said that Greggie was a good Scot. He would be able to pick out a good plaid ribbon.

The bottle of perfume and the plaid ribbon were on

the breakfast table at Merry's place. There was a plaid belt to match the ribbon, from Greggie. Uncle Bill had bought her some plaid socks and Aunt Helen gave her a little jewelry box.

When Jerry came down to breakfast, he said, "I have a present for you, Merry. I'll have to give it to you this afternoon. It isn't finished yet. I have to work on it this morning."

"Don't you want to go on the picnic with Aunt Helen and me?" asked Merry.

"No," said Jerry, "I have a lot of work to do."

Merry saw Aunt Helen wink at Jerry. Jerry looked as though he were keeping a secret.

"Something's up, Merry!" said Uncle Bill. "I can tell. Something's up!"

Everybody laughed. Aunt Helen said, "You had better go or you will miss your train."

Uncle Bill looked at his watch. He jumped up. He ran around the table and kissed Aunt Helen and the children. "So long, Merry Primrose!" he called. "See you later!"

By eleven o'clock the picnic basket was packed. Aunt Helen put it in the back of the car. She and Merry sat on the front seat.

"Is it very far?" asked Merry.

"No," replied Aunt Helen, "it isn't very far. We are going to a place that belongs to a friend of Uncle Bill's. He owns two hundred and seventy-five acres of land."

"What does he do with so much land?" asked Merry.

"Some of it is farm land," said Aunt Helen. "Part of it has been made into gardens. But we are going to the woods."

"Are his woods nicer than the woods back of our house?" asked Merry.

"Oh, my, yes!" said Aunt Helen. "When we get there you will see why."

Aunt Helen turned the car in at a gate with white posts. The curved drive went up a hill. At the top of the hill there was a big stone house.

"Does Uncle Bill's friend live in that house?" asked Merry.

"Yes," answered Aunt Helen, "but he is away."

They drove past the house and around past some greenhouses. At last they stopped in front of a little cottage.

"Why, this looks like an English cottage!" said Merry.

"Yes, it does," said Aunt Helen, "and English people live in the cottage. This is where Brooks, the gardener, lives."

Just as the car stopped a man came out of the cottage. Merry thought he looked like the postman who used to bring the mail to Heartford Square.

"Good morning, Mrs. Hobson," he said. "I thought I heard the car."

"Good morning, Brooks," said Mrs. Hobson. "This is Merry Ramsay."

"Well, I'm glad to know you, Merry," said Brooks. "I hear you are going to the woods for a picnic."

"How do you do," said Merry.

"I'll show you the way," said Brooks.

Brooks led the way. They went past a rock garden and across the green lawn. Merry could see the trees of the woods ahead. As they entered the woods Merry stood still. She gave a little gasp. She could hardly believe her eyes. There under the trees were yellow primroses. They weren't like a carpet, as in England, but as far as she could see there were little clumps of primroses.

"Why, Aunt Helen," she gasped, "they're primroses!"

"Yes, dear one," said Aunt Helen, "primroses."

"But I thought they didn't grow in America," said Merry.

"They don't grow wild," said Brooks; "but I got these plants from England and I planted them here in the woods. I've nursed them along and every year they come up again. They take a deal of nursing though."

"Oh," said Merry, "I don't suppose you ever pick them."

"Oh, yes," said Brooks, "you can pick them. Pick all you want."

Merry was so happy her face shone like the sun. She knelt down and began to pick the primroses. Brooks went off to attend to his work and Aunt Helen sat down under a tree. She took out her knitting.

Merry went from one clump to another, picking

primroses. When she had gathered a large bunch, she said, "I don't think I'll pick any more. I should leave some because they make the woods look so pretty."

"Yes," said Aunt Helen. "I think you have gathered enough. Suppose we eat our lunch now?"

Merry sat down beside Aunt Helen while she unpacked the basket. "Now I can make a primrose chain," said Merry.

Between bites of her sandwiches, Merry fastened the primroses together. "I don't think there are enough to make two chains," she said. "It takes an awful lot of primroses to make a chain."

"Well, just make one chain for yourself," said Aunt Helen.

"Oh, no!" said Merry. "I want to make one for you too."

Merry puckered up her brow and looked at the flowers. "I know," she said; "I'll make bracelets. Bracelets won't take so many flowers. Would you like to have a bracelet, Aunt Helen?"

"Yes, indeed," replied Aunt Helen. "I think a bracelet would be lovely."

Merry worked busily at her bracelets. It was slow work. When she finished, she had some flowers left. "Oh, Aunt Helen!" she cried, "I'm going to have enough to make a bracelet for Molly too."

By the time Merry finished her third bracelet it was two o'clock.

"Now we must go," said Aunt Helen.

Merry fastened one of the bracelets on Aunt Helen's arm. Then Aunt Helen fastened one on Merry's arm. "Aren't they beautiful?" said Merry.

"Indeed they are," replied Aunt Helen.

At the cottage she showed them to Brooks. "They are very pretty indeed," he said.

"It has been just like home," said Merry. "Thank you for letting me pick your primroses."

"Ah!" said Brooks. "It's good to have a little English lass picking primroses. It's as you say, 'just like home.' "

On the way back Aunt Helen said, "Now we will pick up Molly and take her home with us for tea."

When they reached the Prices', Molly came running out.

"Look, Molly!" cried Merry. "I've brought you a primrose bracelet."

"Oh, isn't it pretty!" said Molly, as Merry fastened it on her arm. "Thank you," she said. "I thought there weren't any primroses in America."

Molly climbed into the car. As they drove home Merry told her about the English gardener and the primroses. While she talked Merry noticed that Molly had a little package in her hand. She wondered what was in the package but she was too polite to ask. When they reached Aunt Helen's, Molly and Merry jumped out and ran into the house.

Merry called, "Oh, Jerry! Jerry, where are you?"

"Maybe he's in the library," said Molly.

The two little girls ran into the library. Suddenly the room was full of boys and girls. They jumped out from behind doors and from behind every chair. They all shouted, "Merry Primrose! Merry Primrose!"

There were Nancy and Bobby Brown and the twins, Tommy and Freddy. There was a little girl whose name was Susie and another named Patsy. They were all from school.

Merry was so surprised she couldn't stand up. She sat right down on the floor. All of the children had packages for her. They came and put them in her lap. When Bobby gave her his package, he said, "Say, Merry, I'm awfully sorry I made fun of you, 'cause I like you a lot."

"I like you too," said Merry; "only I didn't at first. I guess I like everybody now."

Merry was delighted with her presents. Now she knew what had been in the package that Molly had held in her hand in the car. It was a little silver thimble.

Jerry had made a sewing-box for her. He was very proud of it. That very morning he had painted it

bright red. He carried it very carefully because he wasn't certain that it was dry. Merry thought it was a lovely sewing-box.

She had never had so many presents before. There was a string of beads from Nancy and a whole dozen new pencils from Freddy. Tommy gave her a box of paints. Susie had brought her a box of notepaper. When she opened the last package, it was a pincushion with a doll sticking right out of the center. It was a present from Patsy.

After Merry had thanked everyone for her presents, the children played games.

At five o'clock Mrs. Hobson took them out into the dining room. At Merry's place there was a beautiful birthday cake with yellow candles. It had white icing and little yellow flowers that looked like primroses. Across the top there were yellow letters that said "Merry Primrose." Even the ice cream was yellow and white. It was vanilla and orange ice.

Merry had never had such a lovely party. She forgot all about the unhappy days that she had known.

That night, before she went to bed, she wrote a letter to her mummy and daddy. She thanked them for her presents and told them all about her surprise Primrose Day.

CHAPTER 7

A LITTLE BLUE PIGEON

ONE MORNING very early Jerry came running into Merry's room. "Hey, Merry!" he said, in a very excited voice. "Merry, wake up!"

Merry rolled over and pulled the covers over her head.

"Merry! Merry!" said Jerry, shaking her. "Wake up."

Merry rubbed her eyes. "What is it?" she asked sleepily.

"Merry, there's a pigeon on the roof outside of my window," said Jerry.

"Well, I've seen pigeons," murmured Merry with her eyes closed. "I've seen lots of pigeons." And she rolled over and buried her face in the pillow.

"But, Merry," said Jerry, shaking her again. "You've never seen this kind of a pigeon before. I'll bet you anything you never have."

"What kind of a pigeon is it?" mumbled Merry with her eyes still shut.

"It's a carrier pigeon," shouted Jerry. "A real carrier pigeon."

Merry's eyes flew open and she sat bolt upright. "A carrier pigeon?" she gasped.

"Yes," answered Jerry. "He's sitting on the roof and he must be awful tired because he looks all droopy."

By this time Merry was out of bed. In another moment the two children were looking out of Jerry's window. "See how droopy he looks," said Jerry. The pigeon did indeed look droopy. He sat hunched up with his head lowered and his eyes closed.

"Oh," said Merry, "the poor little pigeon. He must have flown a long way. Are you sure he's a carrier pigeon, Jerry?"

"Of course he's a carrier pigeon," said Jerry. "Don't you see the little capsule that holds the message? It's fastened to his leg."

"Oh, yes!" exclaimed Merry. "I see it. Oh, isn't it exciting? Do you suppose there is a message in the capsule?"

"Sure there is," replied Jerry.

"Don't you wish you could know what it says? I'll bet it's something very important. Something about the war, I'll bet."

"Or about spies," said Jerry. "I'll bet anything it's about spies."

"Maybe the pigeon is hungry," said Merry. "Maybe he hasn't had anything to eat for days and days."

"Well, let's get him something to eat," said Jerry.

Without waiting to dress, the children padded down the back stairs in their bare feet. Sarah was in the kitchen. She was just starting the breakfast. "Land sakes!" said Sarah. "What do you mean by coming downstairs in your nightclothes? And in your bare feet too!"

"There's a carrier pigeon on the roof, Sarah, right outside my window," said Jerry. "And he's hungry and we want to give him something to eat."

"How do you know he's hungry?" said Sarah. "If you start feeding every pigeon that lights on the roof, you'll have pigeons all over the place. And I don't like pigeons."

"But this is a very special pigeon," said Merry. "It's a carrier pigeon."

"Well, I hope he carries himself off," said Sarah.

"Ah, Sarah, if you could see him, you would feel sorry too," said Merry. "He's so tired and he's all droopy."

"Do you think he would like some cornflakes?" asked Jerry.

"Well, I know they like corn," said Sarah. "So maybe they like cornflakes."

Jerry poured some cornflakes out of the box into a saucer. "Maybe we better take some pieces of bread too," he said.

Merry opened the bread box and took out a piece of stale bread. Then the children started up the back stairs.

"Now see that you don't spill those cornflakes all over the steps," said Sarah.

The children ran up the stairs with the bread and the cornflakes. Jerry opened the window and threw a handful of cornflakes out on the roof. The pigeon didn't budge. Merry broke up the slice of bread and threw the pieces out. Still the pigeon didn't move. They waited quietly, hoping that he would open his eyes. He was as still as a statue.

Jerry ran to the head of the back stairs. "Sarah," he called, "he won't eat the cornflakes or the bread."

"Well, ask him if he would like to have a cup of coffee," said Sarah.

This made the children laugh so hard that Jerry's father came out into the hall to see what the noise was about.

"Oh, Father," cried Jerry, "come and see the carrier pigeon. He's a real carrier pigeon 'cause he has a capsule on his leg."

"A capsule with a message in it," said Merry. "Jerry and I think it's a message about the war or spies or something. Isn't it exciting?"

Mr. Hobson went with the children to look at the pigeon. "Sure enough," he said. "He's a carrier pigeon all right. He has been on a long flight and he's all tuckered out."

"He won't eat anything," said Jerry.

"He will eat when he feels like it," said Mr. Hobson. "He might like some corn. I'll bring some home with me tonight."

Merry ran off to her room to dress. She could hardly wait to go to school to tell the other children about the pigeon. During breakfast the two children talked of nothing else.

"Do you think you could bring him in the house, Father?" asked Jerry. "Do you think we could read the message that he is carrying?"

"I don't believe so," said Mr. Hobson. "It wouldn't be very honorable to read a message that was not meant for us."

When Merry and Jerry got on the school bus, they both talked at once about the carrier pigeon. The children listened to every word.

"Say, can I come see it?" asked Bobby Brown. "I've never seen that kind of a pigeon. Will you let me come and see it?"

"Sure," said Jerry. "But you mustn't frighten him 'cause he's tired and he has to rest."

When the children reached the school, they were all talking about the pigeon. They told Miss Miller about it and she had a nature lesson about carrier pigeons. She told the children about the pigeons that are trained in the army to carry messages. She told them that they were the most certain way to send messages. "You see," she said, "radio messages can be picked up by the enemy. Telegraph lines can be broken and telephone wires can be cut. Messengers can be captured but the pigeon can nearly always carry his message through without fail."

The children's eyes were glued to their teacher's face. "There are pigeons that are trained to fly by night and others that are trained to fly by day," she said.

Peter Morrison raised his hand. "Yes, Peter," said Miss Miller.

"My daddy told me that army pigeons are always a dark color. They are always gray or brown or blue, but they are never white," said Peter. "Do you know why they are never white, Miss Miller?"

"I think it would be nice if you would tell us why they are never white, Peter," said Miss Miller.

"Well," said Peter, "you see, hawks are always after the pigeons. Hawks are very mean birds and they kill the pigeons. Well, the hawks can see the white pigeons but they can't see the dark ones very well. So that is the reason why they don't train white pigeons to be carrier pigeons."

"Our pigeon is a blue one," said Jerry. "I'll bet it is an army pigeon."

"Gee! Wouldn't you like to know what the message says?" said Bobby.

"Father says it wouldn't be honorable to read a message that was meant for someone else," said Jerry. "But I would like to know what it is too."

For days the pigeon sat on the roof. It seemed as though he never moved. The corn that Jerry put out for him wasn't touched. Every day Merry and Jerry brought children home with them from school to see the pigeon.

One day when they came home, the pigeon was walking around the roof. "He's better!" cried Jerry. "The pigeon is better. Look, Merry, he's eating some of the corn."

As the days passed, the pigeon grew more friendly. The children would coax him with corn. At last one day he came and sat on Jerry's hand and ate some of

the corn. Jerry was so delighted he could hardly hold still. That evening the pigeon came to Jerry's father and ate out of his hand. Mr. Hobson was able to see that the number on the capsule was No. 182. He put out his finger to touch the capsule and the bird flew from him. "You see, Jerry," said his father, "the pigeon knows that he hasn't reached the place where he is to deliver the message."

"He's a wonderful pigeon, isn't he, Father?" said Jerry.

"I wish we could keep him," said Merry.

One morning when Jerry looked out of the window the pigeon was gone. Jerry ran over to Merry's room. "Merry," he cried, "the pigeon is gone."

Merry jumped out of bed and ran into Jerry's room. Sure enough, there was no pigeon in sight. "Oh, dear!" sighed Merry. "I'll miss him so much."

"Well, I guess he had to go on with the message," said Jerry. "The people who were waiting for the message must have thought he was lost. I just wish I knew what the message said."

"I'll bet it was about spies. Something very, very important," said Merry.

"Oh, sure!" said Jerry.

A week after the pigeon had left, Mr. and Mrs. Hobson took Jerry and Merry to visit Jerry's grandfather. He lived at the seashore. When they arrived, Jerry told his grandfather all about the carrier pigeon. Grandfather listened to every word. When Jerry finished, his grandfather said, "You know, there is an army fort not far from here where they train carrier pigeons. How would you like to go over there with me and see them? The officer in charge is a friend of mine."

The children's faces beamed. "Oh, Grandfather," said Jerry, "that would be wonderful!"

The next afternoon Jerry's grandfather set off with the two children for the fort. When they reached the fort, the children were surprised to see the low wooden buildings.

"I thought you said it was a fort, Grandfather," said

Jerry. "This doesn't look like a fort. I thought forts were made of stones and were high and had guns on top of them."

"And guns sticking out all around them," said Merry.

"Oh, they are the forts they used to have," said Grandfather. "This is a new kind of fort."

Soon they reached the low white buildings where the pigeons were kept. The officer in charge greeted Jerry's grandfather and the two children. Then he took them to see the pigeons and told them how they were being trained. "We thought one of the pigeons was lost a week or so ago," he said. "I have a pet one of my own. He is a two-way flier. That means that he can fly with a message and come back with one. Some pigeons can only fly home, you know. But this pigeon is very smart and a friend of mine and I have a lot of fun sending messages to each other. My friend is in an army camp about a thousand miles from here. About three weeks ago I sent the pigeon off with a message and he should have been back in a few days. I watched for him but he didn't return. I was a little worried because we had a very bad storm. Two weeks passed and still there was no sign of him. Then one day he flew in. I don't know where he could have been. I wish he could have told me."

Jerry's and Merry's eyes grew rounder and rounder as the officer told about the pigeon.

"Why, there was a carrier pigeon on our roof for almost two weeks," said Jerry. "I wonder if it was your pigeon."

"Well, come and see if he looks like the pigeon that was on your roof," said the officer.

He led the way to the pigeons' roost. "Here he is," said the officer, pointing to a blue pigeon.

"That looks like him," said Jerry. "I remember his number was 182."

"He is the bird, then," said the officer. "He's the very one who was on your roof."

"What was the message?" asked Merry.

"Was it about spies?" said Jerry.

The officer laughed. "No," he said, "it wasn't about spies. I'll let you read it if I still have it in my pocket."

He felt in his pocket and pulled out a little piece of paper all rolled up. It was just big enough to fit inside of the capsule. He handed it to Jerry. When Jerry unrolled it, this is what he read. "Hello, Jerry! This bird is getting so good he will soon be able to fly over with a blueberry pie."

Jerry and Merry laughed at the message about blueberry pie.

"But why does it say, 'Hello, Jerry'?" asked Jerry.

"Well, you see my name is Jerry," said the officer.

"That's funny," said Jerry. "So's mine."

CHAPTER 8

LUNCH IN A TREE-HOUSE

ONE MORNING in June Molly came running into school. She was bursting with news. She rushed up to Miss Miller. "Miss Miller!" she said. "Miss Miller! What do you think?"

"Why, good morning, Molly," said Miss Miller.

"Oh, good morning," said Molly. "I've got the most wonderful news, Miss Miller."

"Well, let's hear it," said Miss Miller.

Molly's eyes were dancing. "Well," she said, "last Saturday Mrs. Price took me to visit a friend of hers.

Her name is Mrs. Carter and she lives way out in the country. Her house is right by a stream of water and there is a boat and in the woods there is a tree-house."

"What's a tree-house?" said Bobby Brown.

"Oh," said Molly, "it's wonderful! It's a play-house built up in the branches of a big tree. You have to climb up a ladder. And Mrs. Carter says we can all come some Saturday and have a picnic. The whole class and you too, Miss Miller. Isn't that wonderful?"

All of the children in the room had crowded around Molly and Miss Miller. When they heard the word "picnic," broad grins spread over their faces.

"When can we go, Miss Miller?" asked Bobby. "I want to see that tree-house."

"So do I," shouted the rest of the children. "When can we go?"

Miss Miller laughed. "You will have to give me time to think about this," she said. "I will have to find out from Mrs. Price just how far away it is. Then, too, I don't know how I could get all of you out there."

"Oh, that's easy," said Freddy. "We could go in my daddy's station-wagon. Shall I ask him, Miss Miller?"

"My daddy has a truck," said Peter.

"My mother would take some of us," said Jerry. "I know she would."

Just then the bell rang for school to begin. "Now take your seats, children," said Miss Miller. "I'll think about the picnic and see whether it is possible for us to go. It was lovely of Mrs. Carter to invite us."

At recess time Bobby said, "Have you thought about the picnic, Miss Miller?"

"No, Bobby, I haven't. But you must have thought about it all morning, for all of your examples are wrong."

Bobby's face grew very red. "I want to see that tree-house," he said.

The next morning the children came to school full of ideas. One after the other rushed into the room, shouting, "Miss Miller, my mother says she will drive some of us to the picnic."

When Freddy arrived, he said, "Didn't I tell you? We can go to the picnic in our station-wagon. My daddy says so."

"Now can we go?" the children cried.

"Well," laughed Miss Miller, "I suppose so."

"Hurrah!" shouted the children.

"Yippie!" cried Bobby.

"Bobby," said Miss Miller, "there will be no picnic for you if you don't get your examples right."

Bobby sat down and began working on his examples.

The following Saturday the children gathered at the school about ten o'clock. Lined up in the drive were Freddy's father's station-wagon and Peter's father's truck. There were also the three automobiles that belonged to some of the parents of the other children. There was plenty of room for everyone. By half-past ten they were on their way. The children held their lunch boxes on their laps. They chattered and laughed and sang all the way to the Carters'.

When they arrived, the very first thing they wanted

to see was the tree-house. Molly led the way. They crossed the bridge to the other side of the stream. Now they were on the edge of the woods. They scuffed their feet through the fallen leaves. In a few minutes Molly stopped. "Here it is," she cried, pointing to a very tall tree. "Only four at a time can go up."

In a moment four children were climbing the ladder that led up to the platform that was laid between the branches of the tree. Bobby was the first one up. "Oh!" he shouted, as he leaned over the railing that formed the side of the house, "this is wonderful!"

Merry was the second one to reach the platform. "Oh, my! It's high!" she said. Then Jerry arrived. He looked down through the leaves at the stream below. "This is like being up on the mast of a ship," he said.

"Move over," said Tommy as he arrived at the top of the ladder. "Give a fellow some room."

"Now shut the gate," shouted Molly from below.

Bobby and Merry shut the wooden gate that closed the entrance to the tree-house. They felt safe and snug

and very far away from the ground.

"Now I know how a bird feels in a nest way up in a tree," said Merry.

"It feels nice," said Bobby. "I would like to be a bird and live in a tree."

In a few minutes Miss Miller called to the children to come down. When they reached the ground, four more children went up. As the children came down, they went into Mrs. Carter's house and put on their bathing suits. It was still warm enough to go in bathing. Some of the children swam while others paddled in the stream. They took turns playing in the rowboat. One or two of the boys could row a little. They took the other children for boat rides.

After all of the children had visited the tree-house, they began to unpack their lunch boxes. Freddy and Tommy and Sally and Nancy scrambled into the rowboat with their lunch boxes. They thought it would be fun to eat their lunch in the boat.

Just then, Merry called down from the tree-house.

"Miss Miller," she shouted, "may we eat our lunch up here?"

Miss Miller looked up into the tree. There were Merry and Molly and Jerry and Peter looking down. "May we, Miss Miller?" they shouted.

"I don't know how you can get your lunches up there," said Miss Miller. "You can't carry them up the ladder."

"Mine is in a basket," said Molly. "And we have a piece of string that we can let down. If you will tie the basket on the string, we can haul it up."

The children down below thought this would be great fun. One of them scampered off to find Molly's basket.

Jerry tied a stick on the end of the string and threw it down. Then Miss Miller tied the basket on the end of the string. "All right!" she called. The children up above pulled the string and the basket left the ground. It swung out over the water. Up, up, up it went. Nearer and nearer it came to the tree-house. At last it reached the children and Molly took her lunch out of the basket. Then they let it down again and one of the little girls put Merry's lunch in the basket.

"Go ahead!" she shouted to the children. Again the basket swung out over the water. Higher and higher it went until it reached the tree-house. Merry unpacked her sandwiches and cookies. Down came the basket again and once more it was packed. This time it was Peter's lunch.

"Hey!" shouted Jerry, "put mine in too. I'm hungry."

"Very well," said Miss Miller, "but it makes a very full basket."

When the basket was lifted from the ground, it was bulging. Out over the water it dangled from the end of the string. Up, up, up it went. "It's heavy," cried Peter. The children down below watched it as it neared the tree-house. All of a sudden the string broke. Basket, sandwiches, hard-boiled eggs, tomatoes, cookies, apples, and oranges flew in all directions and then landed in the water.

"Oh! Oh!" screamed the children. One of the boys waded out into the stream and brought back the basket and an orange. The rest was lost.

Peter and Jerry looked very sad as they watched their lunch float down the stream.

"Never mind," said Merry and Molly; "we'll give you some of ours."

"We all will," shouted Miss Miller. "That is, if you

can mend the string."

Soon the string was mended and the children tied the basket on again. They had great fun putting surprises in the basket. Peter and Jerry never knew what was coming up in the basket. Sometimes it was a sandwich or a cookie. Sometimes it was a piece of cake or some fruit. In the end the two little boys had a great deal more than they could eat.

When the children finished their lunch, it was time to go home. The automobiles had come back for them. The boys and girls picked up all of the papers and boxes and put them in a big can. When they finished, there was one large lunch box at the foot of a tree. Miss Miller looked at the box and saw Bobby Brown's name written on the lid.

"Bobby!" she called, "come pick up your box."

Bobby was nowhere to be seen. The children began to call, "Bobby! Bobby! Miss Miller wants you." There was no reply.

Miss Miller lifted the lid of the box. There was

Bobby's lunch, just as he had brought it. There were sandwiches, gingerbread, crackers and eggs, tomatoes, a bunch of grapes, a cinnamon bun, and two pieces of molasses candy.

"Has anyone seen Bobby?" asked Miss Miller.

"No," replied the children, "not for a long time."

"We will have to hunt for him," said Miss Miller.

They all started off, calling, "Bobby! Bobby! Bobby Brown!"

Miss Miller went across the stream toward the barn. "Bobby!" she called. "Bobby!" There was no answer. She looked all through the barn. Bobby was nowhere to be seen. She could hear the children on the other side of the stream calling, "Bobby! Bobby Brown!"

Just then she heard a knocking. She stood still and listened. It sounded like someone kicking against a wooden fence or wall. Miss Miller went around the side of the barn and there she found a wooden tool shed. Miss Miller ran and opened the door. Out rushed Bobby, straight into Miss Miller's arms. He was crying. Miss Miller sat down on the grass with Bobby. "It's all right, Bobby," she said. "We wouldn't go without you."

"I went in to look at the tools and the door blew shut," sobbed Bobby. "I couldn't open it."

The children gathered around Miss Miller and Bobby. After a few minutes Bobby stopped crying. "I haven't had any picnic," he said.

"Well, your lunch is here," said Miss Miller. "You can eat it in the car, driving home."

When Bobby heard this, he began to cry harder than ever.

"But I wanted to eat it in the tree-house," he cried. "I wanted to eat it in the tree-house."

"Couldn't we play a little longer, Miss Miller?" said Merry. "Just until Bobby eats his lunch in the tree-house?"

"Very well," said Miss Miller.

All of the children ran across the stream and Bobby climbed up the ladder. Merry put his lunch in the basket and Bobby hauled it up. He sat and munched his sandwiches while the children played hide-and-seek. Miss Miller sat at the foot of the tree-house and knitted.

After a while Bobby called down, "Miss Miller, I think I would like to be a bird and live in a tree."

"You do, Bobby?" said Miss Miller.

"Yes," said Bobby, "only I wouldn't like to eat worms and slugs."

"No, I'm sure you wouldn't," said Miss Miller.

Bobby was very quiet while he finished his lunch. When he swallowed the last mouthful, he shouted, "Miss Miller, do you know what kind of a bird I would like to be?"

"I haven't an idea," replied Miss Miller.

"I would like to be a bird that just eats cinnamon buns. I'm coming down now. I'm glad I didn't miss the picnic."

CHAPTER 9

A FISH STORY

When school closed, Mr. and Mrs. Hobson took Merry and Jerry to spend two weeks on a farm. Jerry had spent part of each summer on the farm and he talked of nothing else for days before school closed.

"You'll like the farm, Merry," he would say. "There are chickens and ducks and horses and cows. I can milk a cow. I'll teach you how to milk a cow, Merry. And there is a barn to play in and a stream. The stream is wonderful. That is where we go swimming and where Daddy and I go fishing."

"Is it very deep?" asked Merry.

"No, it isn't very deep. It's deep enough for a row-boat but it isn't deep enough to drown," said Jerry. "I'll take you fishing, Merry. Have you ever been fishing?"

"No," answered Merry. "But I would love to go fishing. It must be fun to catch fish."

"I'll row the boat," said Jerry.

The children spent the first day on the farm exploring. Jerry felt very important as he showed everything on the farm to Merry.

The second day they decided to go fishing. They had each brought a fishing line and they could hardly wait to get out in the boat to fish. Very early in the morning they began digging for worms. They turned up the earth and dropped the worms into an empty tomato can. When the can was almost full, Jerry said, "I think we have enough bait; let's go fishing now."

As the children were leaving, Jerry's father said, "You'll remember not to take the boat past the big rock, won't you, Jerry?"

"Yes, Daddy, I'll remember," said Jerry.

Jerry led the way to the stream. "We never take the boat beyond the big rock," he said, "because there are rapids below."

Soon they reached the stream. There was a green rowboat tied to the little dock.

"Now the best place to catch fish," said Jerry, "is

down the stream, right near the big rock." Jerry pointed down the stream.

"Are you sure you can row the boat?" asked Merry.

"Sure!" said Jerry. "I could almost row it last year."

The children untied the rope and climbed into the boat. Merry sat in the back and Jerry sat in the center. He put the can of bait under the seat. Then he picked up the oars and placed them in the oar-locks. He took hold of the oars and pushed on them with all of his might. The oars lifted a bit. Then Jerry pulled on them. The water splashed. Jerry tried it again. The boat just rocked.

"Do you think you can do it, Jerry?" asked Merry.

"Sure," said Jerry, "it's easy."

He pushed and pulled some more, but the boat stayed by the dock.

"Merry, you push against the dock," said Jerry.

Merry reached out and pushed against the dock. The boat glided away.

"See," said Jerry, "it's easy."

Jerry worked at the oars with all of his strength. He stirred up the water and rocked the boat. "It's a little hard at first to get going," he said.

He worked hard for another five minutes. By this time the boat was back against the dock.

"Give her another push, Merry," said Jerry.

Merry pushed against the dock again. The boat went forward.

"That's great!" shouted Jerry. "Now we're going."

"Splash, splash!" went the oars. The boat began to go around and around like the hands of a clock.

"Well," said Jerry, "suppose we start fishing."

"But I thought we were going to row down the stream," said Merry.

"We don't have to," replied Jerry. "We can catch fish right here."

"But you said the fishing was better down farther," said Merry.

"I know," said Jerry. "But the fish have to go past here to get down there. We might as well catch 'em here."

Jerry lifted the oars into the boat. Then the children unfastened their fishing lines. Jerry lifted the lid on the can of worms. He took out a worm and put it on his hook. Then he dropped the line over the side of the boat.

Merry picked up the can and looked at the worms. She wondered how she could ever get one of those slippery worms on her hook. She felt that she could never pick it up with her fingers. Merry looked around the bottom of the boat. There was a little twig. She picked it up and stuck it in the can. She held her breath while she hung the worm on the hook. Then, "Plop!" went the worm into the bottom of the boat.

Merry leaned over and put the twig under the worm. She lifted it up very slowly. Once more she hung it on the hook. Just as she was about to drop the line over the side of the boat, "Plop!" went the worm down into the water.

"Jerry, how do you make the worm stay on the

hook?" said Merry. "Mine slides off all the time."

"You stick the hook through the worm, silly," said Jerry.

"Right through the worm?" cried Merry.

"Sure," said Jerry.

"Oh, Jerry!" cried Merry. "I can't stick the hook through the worm. It will hurt it."

"No, it won't hurt it," said Jerry. "The worm doesn't feel it."

"Well, I can't put a hook through a worm," said Merry. "I'm going to tie it on."

"Gee, that's just like a girl," said Jerry. "Even have to make bows out of worms."

Jerry felt a little tug on his line. "Oh, boy! I think I've got a nibble," he said.

While Jerry looked after his nibble, Merry lifted another worm out of the can with her little twig. She laid it on the seat beside her. With the twig in one hand and the hook in the other, she tried her best to tie the worm on the hook. It was no use.

"I think I've got one!" cried Jerry, pulling up his line.

Sure enough, flapping on the end of the line was a little fish. Jerry caught it in his hand and took it off the hook. Merry watched him as he laid the fish in the bottom of the boat.

"It's an awful little fish," said Merry.

"Well, it's a fish anyway," said Jerry. "You haven't even got the worm on your hook. I think you're just afraid to pick up the worm."

"I am not afraid," said Merry. "I picked up a grass snake once."

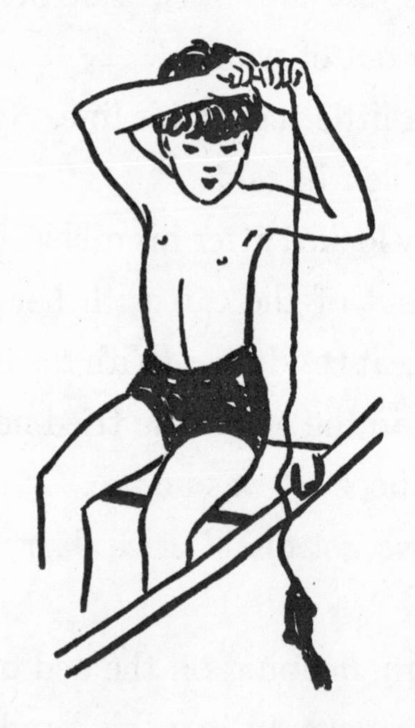

Merry looked at the worm and the hook and the fish. Then when Jerry wasn't looking, she pushed the worm back into the can and dropped her line over the side of the boat.

"So you got it on at last!" said Jerry.

Merry made no answer. She just watched her line.

The two children were quiet a long time. Once Jerry said, "Had any nibbles?"

"Not yet," answered Merry.

After a while Merry said, "I don't think there are any fish here."

"Maybe we should go down the stream," said Jerry, "down where Daddy and I catch them."

"But you can't row the boat," said Merry.

"Sure I can row the boat," said Jerry. "Didn't you see me get it away from the dock?"

Jerry hauled in his line. "Come on," he said, "haul in your line. We're going down the stream."

Merry hauled in her line. "You lost your bait," said Jerry when he saw Merry's empty hook. "No wonder you couldn't catch anything."

Jerry took hold of the oars again. "Now, here we go," he said.

He splashed the oars in the water and the boat began to go around in a circle. After a few minutes of going around Jerry said, "I tell you, Merry, the most fun is to pole the boat. That's the way I like to do it."

"What do you mean, 'pole the boat'?" asked Merry.

"Well, I'll stand up in the front of the boat and you stand up in the back. Then I'll push with my oar and you push with your oar."

"Oh, I see," said Merry. "In England we call that punting."

Jerry took his place in the front of the boat and Merry stood in the back. They pushed the oars down into the mud and stones that formed the bed of the stream. The boat moved quickly through the water. They went faster and faster. Soon they were far from the dock. Jerry forgot all about the big rock. The boat shot past before he noticed it. Suddenly he saw the rapids ahead. The boat was going very fast. Jerry knew that he must stop the boat. But how? Like a flash a thought came to him. He lifted his oar out of the water and jammed it down with all of his might, right in front of the boat. The boat bumped into the oar with a great big thump.

Just as the boat crashed against the oar, Merry saw Jerry fly into the air. He went right over the top of the oar and down into the water with a terrific splash.

The boat stopped with such a jolt that Merry fell out of the back and there was another splash.

The two children picked themselves up. The water was up to their necks. They were both so surprised to be in the water that at first they didn't say a word. Then Jerry said, "Gee! Gee, I guess we fell out!"

Getting back into the boat was much harder than getting out. The children tipped the boat over so far that the little fish fell out.

"Oh," cried Jerry, "there goes my fish! I've lost my nice fish."

By this time the boat had drifted to a near-by rock. The children climbed on the rock and stepped from the rock into the boat. Merry's fishing line was gone and there was only one oar.

Jerry looked around and saw that the other oar was

still sticking in the mud. He jumped overboard again and swam after the oar.

Merry helped him back in the boat. "It's a good thing we wore our bathing suits," said Merry.

"You bet," said Jerry.

"I guess it's almost time for lunch," said Merry.

"I guess it is," replied Jerry. "I wish I hadn't lost my fish. I was going to get it cooked for my lunch."

"That little fish wasn't big enough to cook," said Merry.

"It was so," said Jerry. "It was a beauty."

"It wasn't any bigger than a sardine," said Merry.

"It was so. It was a beauty," said Jerry. "I'm going to try to catch another one."

By this time they had turned the boat around. When they were well past the big rock, they stopped the boat. Jerry baited his hook and threw his line over.

"It's a shame you lost your fishing line," said Jerry.

"Yes," said Merry, "maybe I could have caught a big fish."

They sat very quietly. After a while Jerry felt a little tug on his line. He pulled it in. Sure enough; there was a good-sized fish on the end.

"Oh, boy!" cried Jerry. "He's a dandy."

Jerry took the fish off the hook and put it in the bottom of the boat.

"I'm hungry," said Merry. "Let's go home now."

"I just want to get one more," said Jerry.

Again he baited his hook. In a few minutes he pulled in another fish. He was delighted.

Just then the children heard Jerry's father calling from the dock. "Jerry!" he called. "Come on in. It's almost time for lunch."

The children took hold of the oars again and poled the boat back to the dock. Jerry's father made it fast and helped the children out.

"Look, Daddy!" shouted Jerry. "Look at my fish!"

"That's great!" said his father. "Did you have a good swim?"

"You bet!" replied Jerry. "It was some swim!"

"How did you get along with your rowing?" asked his father.

"Oh, swell!" said Jerry.

"And how did you like fishing, Merry?" said her Uncle Bill.

"Oh, swell!" said Merry.

"Well, that's a fine catch of fish you have there, Jerry," said his father.

"Oh, Daddy! You should have seen the one that got away," said Jerry. "It was a beauty!"

CHAPTER 10

DADDY'S SCARF

During summer vacation Merry had learned to knit. Aunt Helen had bought her some yarn and knitting needles. Then she showed Merry how to knit a scarf. At first the stitches weren't very even and the knitting looked a little higgledy-piggledy. But Merry was very patient and before long she was able to knit very nicely.

Before school opened, Merry had made a scarf for a British soldier. She felt very proud when Aunt Helen sent it off.

One day Aunt Helen said: "Merry, you will soon have to think about Christmas presents for Mummy and Daddy. They will have to be sent very early this year."

"Oh, Aunt Helen," said Merry, "do you suppose I could knit a scarf for Mummy and one for Daddy?"

"I think it would be lovely, Merry," said Aunt Helen, "but you will have to start knitting right away. They must be finished by the middle of October."

The following day Aunt Helen took Merry into the yarn shop in the village. There she bought the yarn for her mummy's scarf. It was pale yellow.

"I am going to knit it into a scarf for my mummy for Christmas," said Merry to the shopkeeper. "And when it is finished, I'll be back for some yarn for my daddy's scarf."

"I'll be watching for you," said the shopkeeper.

Every evening, before Merry went to bed, she would knit a few inches of her mummy's scarf. It grew very slowly but each night when Merry went to bed it was

a little bit longer.

Merry thought it was very beautiful. It made her think of pale yellow primroses. She knew that it would make Mummy think of primroses too. At last the evening came when Aunt Helen said the scarf was long enough. It was finished. Merry tried it on to see how it looked. She was delighted with it.

"Now I can get the yarn for Daddy's scarf," said Merry.

"Yes," answered Aunt Helen, "we will go to the yarn shop tomorrow after school."

When Merry reached the shop, she said to the shopkeeper: "I would like to have some yarn to knit my daddy's scarf. My mummy's is all finished."

"How nice," answered the shopkeeper. "What color do you want for your daddy's?"

"Oh, it has to be 'Air Force Blue,'" answered Merry. "You see my daddy is very important. He is more than just a flier."

"You don't say!" said the shopkeeper.

"Oh, yes!" said Merry. "My daddy is a very important person. He's a very big help to the King, 'cause he knows so much about the Air Force."

"Well, Well!" said the shopkeeper, as she handed the yarn to Merry.

Merry could hardly wait to get home. She was so anxious to get Daddy's scarf started. "Do you think I'll have it finished in time, Aunt Helen?" she asked.

"You will have to work very steadily," said Aunt Helen. "It won't be long before the middle of October."

Merry knitted every day. The scarf grew longer and longer. The middle of October grew nearer and nearer. At last the scarf grew so long that Aunt Helen measured it with her tape-measure. "Just a few more inches, Merry, and that scarf will be finished," said Aunt Helen.

"And when is the middle of October, Aunt Helen?" asked Merry.

"Next week," replied Aunt Helen.

"I'll be finished in plenty of time, won't I?" said Merry.

"Yes, dear," said Aunt Helen. "We will pack the box together, next week."

The following afternoon Merry came home from school and took out her knitting. Aunt Helen was out and she was alone in the library. Merry began to knit as fast as she could. She was so anxious to finish the scarf. She knitted so fast that she dropped a stitch.

"Oh, dear," she said, "now I've dropped a stitch!"

She tried to pick it up as Aunt Helen had showed her.

Suddenly Greggie dashed into the room. He was so glad to see Merry that he leaped up on her.

"Oh, Greggie," cried Merry, "now see what you have done! My needle has come out of all of my stitches. Now I'll have to wait until Aunt Helen comes. She will have to put them back on my needle."

Merry laid her scarf very carefully on the seat of the big chair. The ball of wool was beside the scarf. Merry went upstairs to her room and got her fairy story book. She curled up in a chair beside the window. She would be able to see Aunt Helen when she drove into the driveway.

Greggie lay at Merry's feet. His head lay between his paws and he rolled his eyes at Merry. He wished she would come and play with him. He thought it was silly to sit so still. It was fun to run and jump and catch balls. Every once in a while Greggie would give a sharp bark. Merry paid no attention. She was off in fairyland. A wicked witch had just turned the beautiful prince into a frog.

Greggie grew tired of watching Merry staring at a book. He didn't know that she was in fairyland. Greggie got up and went downstairs. He wandered from room to room. At last he decided to have a good run around the library. If he ran hard enough he could make the rugs slide. Round and round the room he ran. He ran so fast that he knocked against the chair where Merry's knitting lay. The jolt sent the ball of

yarn to the floor. Greggie stopped running and went to look at the ball of yarn. He smelled it. It smelled very nice. It smelled just like Merry.

Greggie took the ball in his mouth. It felt nice and soft. He thought it was a very fine ball indeed. He decided to take it out of doors.

It was a warm day and the front door was open. Out trotted Greggie with the ball of yarn. The scarf dragged on the ground behind him. Out on the lawn Greggie began to play with the ball. He pushed it with his nose and it rolled along the ground. He worried it and shook it. He growled at it and barked at it. Then he took it in his mouth again and ran the length of the house. The scarf caught on a bush. Greggie ran around the house and into the garden. The scarf unraveled as he ran. The farther Greggie ran, the longer the string of yarn grew from the scarf to the ball. The scarf grew smaller and smaller. Greggie ran all around the bushes and all over the flowerbeds. The blue yarn was soon wound around every bush and plant. It was tangled and snarled.

Just as Aunt Helen drove into the drive, Merry came running out of the front door. Greggie ran to Aunt Helen and dropped the ball of yarn at her feet.

"Oh, Greggie!" cried Aunt Helen and Merry both at once. "Oh, Greggie! What have you done!"

Merry picked up the ball and looked around for Daddy's scarf. She saw the tangled yarn all over the bushes and the flowerbeds. Hanging to one of the bushes was a few inches of Daddy's scarf. Merry could hardly believe her eyes. "Oh, Aunt Helen," she cried. "Aunt Helen, look at my daddy's scarf!"

Merry cried as though her heart would break. Aunt Helen lifted her up and carried her into the house. She sat down in the library and held Merry on her lap. Merry sobbed and sobbed.

"Never mind, darling," said Aunt Helen. "I have a scarf almost finished and you can have it to send to Daddy."

"No, no," cried Merry. "I want him to have one that I have made myself. Just like Mummy's. Now I haven't any Christmas present for Daddy."

When Greggie saw Merry crying, he hid under the sofa. He knew that he had been naughty.

When Uncle Bill came home, he heard the sad story about Daddy's scarf. He did his best to cheer Merry. After dinner he took Merry and Jerry to see a funny motion picture, and for a little while Merry forgot about her daddy's scarf.

The next morning Merry said: "I'm going to knit another scarf for Daddy. I'll write and tell him about Greggie. And I'll tell him that I am making a new scarf."

"I'll buy you some new yarn when I go to market this morning," said Aunt Helen.

When Merry came home from school, she set to work on the new scarf.

When the day came to send the Christmas package off to England, Merry wrapped her mummy's scarf in bright red paper. She wrote on a card, "Merry Christmas to Mummy dear. I wish you and Daddy could be here for Christmas. With love from Merry."

Then she wrote a letter to her daddy. This is what she wrote:

"Dear Daddy,

"I am making a scarf for your Christmas present. I had one almost finished and Greggie ran away with the ball of yarn. He ran all over the garden and pulled out all of my knitting. I am sorry you won't have the scarf for Christmas but I will send it soon. I wish I could see you.

"Love and kisses from

"Merry."

As Christmas drew near, Jerry and Merry talked about the presents they wanted. One evening Aunt Helen said, "Merry, if you could have anything you wanted for Christmas, what would you ask for?"

Merry looked up from her knitting. "Anything at all?" she asked.

"Yes," said Aunt Helen, "anything at all."

Merry thought for a moment. Then she said, "I would like to have my daddy so that I could give him his present."

"Oh, Merry darling!" cried Aunt Helen. "I wish I could give you your daddy for Christmas. I am afraid you will have to tell me something easier than that."

"Well," said Merry, "I would like ice-skates with white shoes."

The day before Christmas the Hobsons' house was bustling with excitement. The children wrapped up their presents and hid them in their bureau drawers. They carried the keys to the drawers in their pockets. Packages of all sizes and shapes were delivered at the front door. Aunt Helen would put them in the hall closet and lock the door.

Sarah was busy in the kitchen, making mince pie

and stuffing the big turkey. The telephone bell rang again and again. It was always Uncle Bill wanting to talk to Aunt Helen. Merry wondered why Uncle Bill had to talk to Aunt Helen so many times. Once she heard Aunt Helen say: "Oh, Bill! How wonderful! I can't believe it! Oh, I do hope it is true! When will you be sure?"

Merry said, "What do you hope is true, Aunt Helen?"

"Oh, something wonderful, Merry," said Aunt Helen. "I can't tell you now."

When Uncle Bill came home to dinner, Aunt Helen ran to the door to meet him. "What have you heard?" she said.

"Nothing certain," replied Uncle Bill.

"Oh, dear," sighed Aunt Helen.

After dinner the children went to bed early so that they could get up early on Christmas morning.

After Merry was in bed, the telephone rang. She heard Uncle Bill say, "Well, hello! My, but it is good to hear your voice!" Then he said "Yes" a lot of times. Before he hung up the receiver he said, "I'll be at the station."

Merry fell asleep wondering why Uncle Bill was going to the station.

After a while Merry heard a voice calling to her. "Merry, Merry darling," the voice said.

Merry opened her eyes. The bright light in the room almost blinded her. She blinked her eyes and looked up. "Daddy! Daddy!" she cried. For there, standing by her bed, was her own daddy.

Daddy took her up in his arms. He wrapped the quilt around her and sat down in the chair by the window. Merry lay with her head against his chest. "Daddy, where did you come from?" she said.

"I came over on a special mission for the government," he said. "I didn't know whether I would get here in time for Christmas. That is why Aunt Helen and Uncle Bill didn't tell you. We didn't want you to be disappointed."

"Oh, Daddy!" said Merry. "It's wonderful! Now I can give you your scarf."

"And we'll go skating," said Daddy, as he kissed his little girl. "You on your skates and I in my scarf."